Turpi

Richard Foreman

Turpin's Shot

Turpin pretended to be asleep, as he sat in the corner of the carriage travelling from Whitechapel to Hempstead. There was already a long list of things, too extensive to count, which bored him in life. He could now pencil - or ink - in the conversation of the journalist, Roderick Helston. Turpin hoped that the man's tiresome voice would send him to sleep in earnest. Helston talked about himself so much, he could have been mistaken for an actor.

The famed highwayman was travelling home, under his alias of John Palmer, from having been in London for a few days. He had met with Joseph Colman to fence several choice pieces of loot. The remainder of the booty, along with the outlaw's pistol and sword, were packed away in his bags, strapped to the back of the carriage. A tricorn hat was tipped forward, covering his darkly handsome but drained features. A large meal, a couple of bottles of porter and the exertions of his latest mistress had fatigued him the night before.

Or perhaps it was leading a double life, or leading a long life of crime, which had exhausted Turpin. The butcher's son had been a pickpocket as a child. Eventually he had joined the Gregory Gang and turned to housebreaking. He then added being a footpad to his crimes, before becoming famous - or infamous - as a highwayman. Crime sold, in relation to the newspapers. Readers lapped up stories about "the age's Robin Hood." There were tales of his female victims swooning. He was purported to be, by one merchant's daughter, "as handsome - and wicked - as the Devil." Turpin had learned his letters, as well as learning how to use a sword, and had quoted poetry and aphorisms whilst relieving people of their valuables. An esteemed periodical described the highwayman as "the finest pistol

1

shot in the county, or country." His name was linked to countless crimes. One newspaper even reported that Turpin had committed robberies in Suffolk and Edinburgh on the same day. The more outlandish the story, the more the reading public believed it.

But stories seldom match reality. Turpin had married and lived a life of seeming respectability, under his alias, as the owner of a tavern and butcher's shop in Hempstead. His domestic routine was as mundane as the next man's. He endured boredom and taxes. Inflation could eat away at him, as well as melancholy. John Palmer was careful rather than fearless. As John Palmer, he endeavoured to blend in. But Dick Turpin lived in the shadow of the gallows. If apprehended, he would be hung quicker than a Grub Street hack could compose his obituary. Black Bess would only be able to outrun his past sins for so long, Turpin sometimes thought. But crime paid - and Turpin continued his career as a highwayman, aided by his friend Nathaniel Gill. Turpin also continued to enjoy the attractions of London. He had even taken lodgings in Charing Cross. Expensive mistresses didn't come cheap. A double life meant twice the expense.

Yet, as much as Turpin reaped the fruits of his labours and was distracted by the pleasures of the capital, he also appreciated returning home. He would just have preferred to do so without suffering the company of a vain glorious journalist. Helston wore a frayed, powdered wig. The writer, a middling talent from the middling classes, was keen to give the impression that he was part of the establishment class which he often wrote about. But his coat and stockings had seen better days, they were more frayed than his wig. His fingers were ink-stained, his shirt wine-stained. Turpin had once admired writers, until he met them. Novelists could make Narcissus appear self-effacing - and journalists never let the truth get in the way of a good commission. The pale faced hack continued to prattle on, as the coach rattled from side to side on the rutted road:

"A picture may be as good as a thousand words, but words can paint a thousand pictures... I sometimes cover the den of iniquity, or din of iniquity, of parliament. Oh, the stories I could tell you. I have witnessed the finest gentlemen in the land resemble pigs, burying their snouts in a trough. I am surprised that they do not run out of knives in the dining room, such is the backstabbing in the place. It's almost the official sport there... I recently interviewed the actress, Pearl Woods. You may have seen the piece, in *The Herald*. She may well be the most unique performer in a generation. She mentioned that she admired my work and she would be in touch with an open invitation to the soirees she puts on each month... If my job has taught me anything, it is that everyone wants to be famous... I am working on a novel, for my sins. I want to portray society as it is, hold a mirror up to it. The protagonist is a journalist, just matriculated from Oxford, who is torn between two women. A colleague mentioned that the writing is reminiscent of Defoe..."

Turpin could partly forgive the fellow's tedious boasts as his ambition was to impress the young woman sitting with them in the carriage. Clara Hambledon. Daughter of Samuel Hambledon, who had concerns in shipping and the silk trade. Helston, who had a nose for a story and for people with wealth and influence, had heard of the affluent merchant. Below the woollen shawl around her shoulders, the nineteen-year-old wore a high-necked, lace-trimmed green dress which bespoke of a modest sensibility. Or perhaps the woman was bored of the looks and leers she generated when she dressed less modestly, Turpin fancied. A small, black satin bonnet was perched at a jaunty angle on her head. An oval face was home to fine blue eyes, a pert nose and a mouth which pouted with a bit too much seriousness and severity for one so young. The blush and bloom of youth was all the make-up she needed. Clara was returning home from a shopping excursion to London (several dresses and hat boxes occupied the carriage, inside and out). A novel, written by Eliza Haywood, lay on the woman's lap, which she often fingered and seemed keen to read, but the lady did not wish to appear impolite. She hoped that the journalist would need to save his voice at some point and cease speaking, but Helston could doubtless talk for as long as Robert Walpole would remain entrenched in office.

"Perhaps you could introduce me to your father at some juncture?" Helston remarked, fishing.

The silence in return spoke volumes and Turpin wryly smiled to himself. He also wrinkled his nose a little, as the pungent smell from the driver's pipe entered the carriage once more, ousting the lady's subtle perfume. The coachman, Jack Brindley, was old rather than ancient. He could still fire the blunderbuss he carried, although it was unknown whether he would still be standing on his feet afterwards. Turpin had encountered plenty of veteran coachmen before, both as a passenger and highwayman. His jokes could sometimes be as dirty as his undercarriage and he could drink for England, or even Scotland, but Brindley was basically a decent man trying to earn an honest living. The coachman's son, Edgar, sat next to him. Scrawny. Callow. Devoted. The father was, quite literally, looking to hand the reins over to his child - teach him his trade.

A storm, the evening before, had uprooted plenty of trees along the way so Brindley thought little of it when he encountered a young elm strewn across the road, obstructing their path. He slowed the coach to a halt, quickly assessed the situation and then called his son down to help him shift the tree, leaving the blunderbuss behind the seat.

The three figures appeared out of the woods like ragged sprites, bracken crackling beneath their boots. The lead figure, clad in brown breeches and a mud-stained black coat, closed in on the carriage as he instructed his two confederates (one carrying a butcher's knife, the other a thick club) to watch the coachmen.

Instinct and/or experience told Turpin that something was amiss, even before the highwaymen broke cover. As soon as he heard the commotion, he was ready to kick a couple of hat boxes aside, exit the carriage and run. He could have disappeared into the treeline and made his escape. Perhaps it was the look of distress on the young woman's face that kept the outlaw in his seat. Turpin was also intrigued as to who was carrying out the robbery on his doorstep.

Turpin heard the familiar sound of a pistol being cocked just before a bearded face appeared at the opposite window - grinning in triumph at first, before grinning with lust as he took in Clara Hambledon. Turpin chose to sheepishly look away rather than challenge the man's gaze. He needed to now play a part, hopefully not that of a corpse by the end of the hour.

"Out!" the man commanded, his voice rough with tobacco and hate.

Helston's pale face grew paler, as he dry-gulped. Turpin tried to offer up a reassuring expression to the terrified woman as he held her trembling hand whilst she alighted from the coach.

The leader of the make-shift gang ordered the coachmen and passengers to line-up at the front of the carriage, a few paces from where the two perspiring mares observed events with blissful indifference, enjoying the respite. Jack Brindley's shoulders and features drooped, by way of an apology for being duped and ambushed in such a manner.

His son could barely turn his attention away from the highwayman's pistol, perhaps fearing that the weapon could flash and kill at any moment. Roderick Helston was speechless, for once. Clara's skin crawled, as she pulled her shawl around her shoulders - and chest - in response to the three criminals ogling her. Turpin appeared wary, but not petrified, like a man who knew that if he just complied then he would live through the unpleasant ordeal.

"My name is Stephen Bryant. You may have heard of me. I've been called a gentleman thief," the highwayman, armed with a pistol, announced in a Norfolk accent. His tone was both playful and hard. "You should almost be honoured that I'm robbing you today. You will have a story more valuable than any trinkets I take off you now."

Turpin had heard of his fellow highwayman. Nathaniel Gill had only spoken about their rival last week.

"The newspapers haven't reported it, but I heard that his gang raped one of the women he held up. Bryant has also killed, just for the fun of it. Apparently, he used to be a schoolteacher. But he was accused - wrongly, he claims, of course - of stealing and he was put in prison for a couple of years. If he didn't go in a criminal, he came out as one. Unfortunately, the bastard is now working on our patch, stirring up trouble. The army will soon be sent out to catch him, but I'm worried they might catch us in the process. God willing he'll come face to face with a coachman's blunderbuss and we can all carry on as normal again," the brawny outlaw remarked - with a ribbon of foam from his beer lining his top lip as he spoke.

Bryant was of medium height, medium build. He possessed pinched features and a striding, confident gait. The default position of his mouth was that of a grin cum sneer. Flinty eyes sat beneath bushy eyebrows.

The younger of his associates was Samuel Bew. Slim, wiry, fidgety and freckled. Strawberry-blond (ginger) hair.

Bew was Bryant's drinking companion turned outlaw, from serving as a carpenter's apprentice, after witnessing the money his friend came into. It was seemingly easy money. Dishonest money. But money was money. The young man could now afford his own lodgings - and didn't now need to pick only the tuppenny whores. He could spend thruppence - or more if flush.

Next to him stood, or swayed from drinking, Tom Drummond. The burly footpad had recently been enjoying his spoils, by eating well each night. Oysters. Mutton. Stews. Pike. Pies. Puddings. Cheeses. Drummond's stomach was at the heart of his character. There was a danger that the buttons on his shirt, stretched across his potbelly, could shoot off faster than a cannonball at any moment, Turpin fancied. Piggy eyes, within podgy features, took in the young woman as Drummond licked his lips and leered. He had a large wart on his chin. A yellowing bruise, from a tavern brawl, marked the left side of his jaw. His aspect - and the blade of his butcher's knife - glinted in the afternoon sun.

"I can help you tell your story, if you want," Helston said, hesitantly - with the idea that the journalist would need to be alive to profile the highwayman. "I can turn you into the next Dick Turpin."

"Turpin? Turpin is a nobody. A common criminal with a famous horse. He'll be forgotten in ten years. But I won't be. And my story should be told. I was unjustly imprisoned. Now I intend to right that wrong, get the money I'm owed from those lost years from the people who can best afford it. I am on a mission, sent from heaven or hell. Turpin is only a name because of scribblers like you, trying to sell newspapers. He's vermin - and I would happily say that to his face if he were here."

Turpin smiled to himself as he listened to the highwayman, who believed in his own press too much, prattle on. He also kept a worried eye, however, on Tom Drummond. The porcine outlaw seemed fixated on the young woman's mother of pearl buttons on her dress, or he was lasciviously imagining what might be beneath them.

"And how are you my lovely? Never mind the coin, I've already got my prize," Drummond remarked, with a gap-toothed grin, moving towards the girl. His eyes bulged, along with another body part. But before the highwayman could reach out and paw the woman Turpin moved in front of Clara to block the approach. The chivalrous act could have also been judged a foolish one, though.

"Be content with the coin, fella," Turpin said, a clear warning emanating from his features and tone. For a moment his fingers tickled the air, reaching for a pistol which he wasn't carrying.

Drummond grunted - and then snarled - before cursing and unleashing a jab, hoping to teach the stranger some manners. But Turpin saw the punch coming. Drummond's flabby hand connected with air, as Turpin punched his opponent in the groin. The gang-member slumped to the ground and dry-retched.

The right thing to do had been a mistake. Turpin saw Bryant raise his pistol - and witnessed a telling look in his eye that he was willing to use it. Turpin ducked and ran at the same time. He heard a click and then the weapon exploded into life, spitting fire and coughing out a cloud of smoke. The bullet struck the door of the carriage, just behind Turpin, as he scrambled towards the rear of the coach.

"Bastard!" Bryant emitted, drool running down his chin. Ungentlemanlike. "You're a dead man. Or a dead dog. Aye, your last act in this life will be to cower and run like a cur. I won't miss a second time," he added, as he fished out another bullet and proceeded to load his weapon.

Clara nearly sobbed. The pistol shot still rang in her ears, quickened her heart. She was worried for the man who had tried to protect her, although the gentlewoman was understandably more concerned for her own wellbeing.

Jack Brindley was tempted to rush the highwayman and try to wrestle the pistol from the rogue. But the coachman needed to protect his boy rather than any foolhardy passenger.

Helston hoped that the thieves would leave the journalist with his notebook and pen, so he could start to write the story up immediately.

Bryant finished loading his pistol. He had received the weapon from a fence in Yarmouth, as part payment from a haul of loot. He breathed in the smell of saltpetre from the previous shot and walked towards the back of the carriage. Bryant was looking forward to seeing the terror in the caitiff's eyes, just before pulling the trigger.

"So, to help our friend here with his story, do you want to give us your name?" the thief, who desired to be mentioned in the same breath as Claude Duval, asked.

The sound of the highwayman's boots crunching upon the ground grew louder in Turpin's ears with each step, to the rhythm of a funeral march.

Hedgerows and leafy trees could be seen in the background, along with lush green fields, sprouting crops and a dimpled stream. Shafts of honeyed sunlight pierced through dove-white clouds. Surely it was too fine an afternoon to die, Turpin might have thought. But what did nature care for the fate of Man? Life and death were as capricious as actresses.

"I'm nobody," Turpin said, as he appeared from behind the coach. Another shot hammered out. The bullet struck him in the shoulder. When the smoke cleared Turpin saw Bryant on the ground, groaning and clutching his wound. Turpin had retrieved his pistol from his bag, which had been strapped to the carriage. The claim that the highwayman was the finest shot in the county could be considered misplaced, as the famed outlaw had aimed for Bryant's chest.

Bew charged, too enraged to be tempered by shock. His club raised in the air above his head, ready to strike. There wasn't time for Turpin to reload his pistol or retrieve Bryant's weapon which lay out of reach underneath the coach. But he did have time to grab his sword from his bag. It was not the first time that Turpin had been attacked by an irked assailant wielding a club. He kept a cool head. He sidestepped the blow and then swiftly and elegantly thrust the point of his sword into the adolescent's thigh, twisting the weapon for good measure. Bew let out a yelp and yowl as he writhed upon the muddy ground like a worm, hooked by a fisherman.

The yowl was soon eclipsed by a rasping yell as Drummond entered the fray, having just about recovered from his eye-watering injury. Turpin parried two savage swipes from the butcher's knife. Drummond moved quickly for a big man. But not quickly enough. Turpin moved inside and punched the stout outlaw with the polished handguard of his finely crafted rapier, splitting open his nose like a rotten tomato. Blood poured into his piggy eyes, blinding him to the boot which Turpin buried in his groin.

Jack Brindley levelled two pistols at the prisoners as Turpin restrained the three men using the straps which he had from fastening the baggage to the coach, trussing them up like pieces of meat.

"Highwaymen, eh? The scum of the roads," the coachman said.

"Perhaps. One should be careful of tarring them all with the same brush, though," Turpin replied.

Clara nearly swooned, from relief. Her honour and purchases were secure. She was tempted to invite her brave, handsome and enigmatic deliverer to dinner, at her father's estate. Turpin would have been tempted to accept, if only to rob the merchant.

Edgar Brindley was now absent from the scene, having been instructed to venture up the road to *The White Hart* tavern, where he would doubtless find some soldiers drinking there. If they wouldn't be compelled by duty to apprehend the highwaymen, Turpin gave the boy some coins to help persuade them.

Roderick Helston scribbled furiously away in his notebook, whilst mulling over which publications would offer him the most money for the story. *Crime pays.* His attention was duly distracted when he noticed that the passenger who had miraculously saved them was appearing to depart. He collected his bags, explaining that he lived close by and would walk the rest of the way home.

"But you cannot leave now. Do you not want to tell your story? I can make you famous," Helston urged, his voice going up an octave in incredulity or desperation. "You must at least let me know your name."

Turpin paused, smiled and replied:

"If I told you, I dare say that you and your readers wouldn't believe it - for once."

The highwayman then thanked the veteran coachman, before trudging home.

Turpin's Dagger

Helion Bumpstead. Essex.

"You wouldn't believe me if I told you, but as sure as my name is George Pine, I rode with Dick Turpin. We were, quite literally, as thick as thieves," the short, bowlegged customer in *The Three Horseshoes* remarked, downing another mouthful of ale, as he conversed with the Grub Street hack. His garb had been presentable once, but the dull brown and grey garments were now worn - marked with patches and poor needlework. Pine had suffered a litany of misfortunes over the years, most of them due to his own weak character. He had debts that no honest, or dishonest, man could pay. Even his own wife didn't trust a word he said. Or his wife especially didn't trust any word that came out of his mouth. His hair was as black as his nails. Often, he would scratch his wiry, scraggy beard. Beady eyes looked out from over a crooked nose.

His nose wasn't the only thing crooked about him, Dick Turpin thought as he sat within earshot of the two men on a nearby table, wryly smiling as he worked his way through another measure of porter. The highwayman had never even seen the fellow before, let alone ridden with him.

It was not the first time that the outlaw had overheard someone in a tavern claim to know him, or spout a rumour about the famous, or infamous, criminal. Everyone had a story about the dandy highwayman - and everyone believed they knew what he looked like. Which Turpin was fine with, as the authorities were now searching for, "A dusky, Moorish half-blood... He's as white as a sheet, with a puckered scar around his neck from where they once tried to hang him... He walks with a limp, from a bullet wound... His hair is brown, with streaks of grey... His locks are fair, like spun gold... His eyes are as blue and still as a becalmed sea... His aspect is dark, eyes as black as those on a shark... I remember him being rake thin... As broad as a barrel... Muscular, like a dock worker... He dresses like a dandy... Like an undertaker, all in black..."

Dick Turpin was everyone and no one. A patchwork of rumours and colourful stories recounted in smoke-filled taverns and London broadsheets. Usually, it proved to be the more far-fetched tales which took root and spread like wildfire. If some of the newspapers were to be believed, the highwayman had killed more folk than the plague and robbed more people than a tax collector.

"So, what is Turpin like?" the young journalist asked, leaning forward on his chair, eager for his goose to lay a golden egg or two. *The Three Horseshoes* was the third tavern he had travelled to in the area, hoping to find someone who knew the notorious outlaw.

"As tough as old leather, but tender when it comes to the ladies. I've witnessed women swoon, even though they can only see his eyes, what with Dick wearing his mask."

Amused rather than angry, that the sot was using his name so freely and falsely, Turpin's wry smile blossomed into a roguish grin as the highwayman continued to listen in on the interview.

"Did you ever meet one of Turpin's mistresses?"

"Aye, there was a pretty piece of an actress. Jane her name was. I think her stage name was Penelope or Persephone. She had a great pair of - lungs. Her voice could reach the back of the theatre, although the fellas in the audience were keen to watch her from the front stalls. Dick tossed her away like a worn horseshoe though once he'd had his fun. It's easy come and easy go, when it comes to money and women for Dick."

The journalist, one Henry Cavendish, continued to enthusiastically take notes. Turpin took in the young man. He cut an elegant figure for a Grub Street hack. His jacket and breeches were new and well-tailored. His clipped, upper-class accent might get him mocked or robbed in less reputable taverns than *The Three Horseshoes*, the highwayman thought. Frilly cuffs adorned a fine linen shirt. It was difficult to keep track of whether they were currently in fashion or not. Cavendish was recently out of university. Already he had mentioned, three times, that he had attended Oxford. No doubt he was trying to make a name for himself as a writer. He wanted to make some money too, but his father still gifted him an allowance so he could afford to live in a salubrious part of London. Despite being new to the profession, Cavendish had already secured a few commissions through his father's connections. Tarquin Cavendish, who owned a shipping company, agreed to place advertisements in the publications that his son wrote for. Turpin thought how the moneylender and fence, Joseph Colman, would have called the overprivileged writer "Blue-bloodied but green."

The conversation and drink continued to flow. Pine's answers only prompted more questions:

"Why do you think that Turpin has, so far, been able to escape capture? Some say he's too wily - or lucky."

"He's both! He's a wolf and a fox. And a badger. There's no finer shot or blade in all of England. There's not a horse in the county, or country, which can match Black Bess either. She's as large as a shire but as sleek as a stallion. You should tell your readers how she loves eating apples. She's a horse sent from heaven, or hell. Dick said he bought her at an auction just outside of Norwich."

"It may not be the authorities who ultimately catch up with him. As I understand, there are rival outlaws who wish to bring Turpin's criminal career to an end. He is rumoured to have killed Owen Blake and his gang, after an encounter on the highway."

"It's no rumour, friend. You might not believe me, but I was there. I saw Dick bring the Blake Gang to the sword. By the end Turpin was covered in blood, from head to toe almost. When someone asked what happened, when they came late to the scene, Dick just replied - "Justice!" Here, he gave me this dagger afterwards," Pine said, retrieving a small, non-descript knife from his coat pocket. "Dick told me that he had carried the blade for years, having held it to more than one of his victim's throats. But he wanted me to have it. It means the world to me. I treasure it. I can't help but think about my old friend when I see it. Do you think that your newspaper would be interested in purchasing the knife?"

By now the two men had gained a small audience. A couple of regulars had ceased playing dice to listen in. A trio of serving girls, who had finished their shift, sat close by and grew increasingly captivated. Essex girls are not averse to enjoying a drink. One of them believed that a patron on a black horse, who visited the tavern last week, could have been the famous highwayman. She thought how she would have slept with him, if he had been more generous in paying for table service. Pine had also attracted the attention of two men, who dressed well enough but appeared a little rough around the edges. They listened intently to Pine's stories and occasionally whispered to one another. Turpin noted how the solidly built figures carried knives and Billy clubs, tucked into the waistbands of their trousers. He couldn't discern the telling bulge of a pistol, but that didn't mean that they were not armed with guns too (as Turpin himself was, along with a sword which hung from his hip).

15

George Pine was now drinking more than steadily, and clearly enjoyed being the centre of attention. He would nod to one of the serving girls to bring him another frothy ale. His voice grew louder, his hands sawed the air as he grew more animated. It was quite a performance, Turpin thought.

But surely the journalist knew that it was a performance too? The hack may have thought that he had struck gold in coming across the self-titled "friend" of the highwayman, but he must have known it was fool's gold? Yet the journalist probably didn't care. He would still be able to argue to a newspaper editor that he was quoting a source. Turpin was unlikely to step forward and give evidence in court, that he was being slandered or libelled. Why let the truth get in the way of a good story? The world wants to be deceived. So let it. Lies are easy to swallow. It's the truth that's often unpalatable.

"He may be called wicked by some, but the Dick Turpin I know is a generous soul. A real gent. This age's Robin Hood. I have seen him give half his booty away, to orphanages. That's the God's honest truth. I swear to you. I remember how he once heard that a local blacksmith was struggling for business, so he went there and bought all the stock and services he could. If Dick was here now, he would buy everyone a drink. Even any Irish folk present. Maybe not the Liverpudlians though."

Turpin pursed his lips and rolled his eyes. Pine was beginning to wear his name out through overuse. The highwayman had initially been amused by the garrulous drunk, but he was now growing bored. Turpin had stopped off at the tavern for a quiet drink or three - and to read the latest issue of *The London Magazine* - but Pine was anything but quiet. As unobtrusively as possible, Turpin picked up his drink and moved to an empty corner of the establishment. The small audience surrounding Pine and his interviewer didn't give him a second look.

Henry Cavendish pursed his lips and rolled his eyes as well as he observed how one of his lace cuffs was lying in a pool of ale on the table. Yet he was still excited by the exclusive material he was gathering. Editors might even enter into a bidding war to pay for the article. Tales of highwaymen helped to sell newspapers. *Crime pays*, the writer thought.

***

Evening.

It was time to venture home, Turpin decided. His wife, a hot meal and a good book awaited. The rumour was that the highwayman spent his nights at the gaming tables, with a courtesan on his lap and a clay pipe in his mouth. But legends can be just as dull and domesticated as the next man.

Turpin left through the side entrance of the establishment. Half the patrons inside were beginning to liven up, partaking in some after work drinks, whilst others sat with their heads buried in their hands. Half asleep or half dying, groaning like their bowels were giant bruises. Turpin came out into a dark alleyway, littered with empty barrels and wooden boxes, smelling of damp, ale and rotting vegetables. He heard the squeal of rutting foxes in the distance. He also heard voices coming from the other end of the alleyway and observed three silhouettes. It was the two Billy club carrying men, with Pine standing in between them. Cornered. His features pinched in fear.

"So, you say that you rode with Turpin, when he took on Blake and his gang?" Ned Butler, the larger of the two men, remarked - before snorting and spitting. He swayed a little and slurred his words, from having one too many drinks. His voice was as rough as his stubble. The former bare-knuckle fighter had cauliflower ears and a nose which had been broken more times that a harlot's heart.

"We once rode with Blake. He was a good friend of ours," his companion, Tom Martin, an equally thuggish looking fellow, added.

"It was just a story," Pine replied, recoiling from smelling Martin's rancid breath. His tone was somewhat shriller and shakier to what it had been when talking to the rapt journalist. He felt like his bowlegs might give way at any moment.

"But you swore it was a true story," Butler asserted, balling his hand into a fist, his knuckles cracking.

"I don't know what happened. That's the God's honest truth. I wasn't there! I swear to you."

"But you're here now, with some coins in your pocket, profiting from telling lies about the death of our friend," Ned Butler remarked, his expression as hard and flat as the brickwork on both sides of the alley.

Pine's heart sank, his complexion grew as pale as the moon, resigned to the fact that he would have to give up his small bounty. He felt like he was being taxed. And tax is a four-letter word. At least losing his hard-earned money was preferable to losing his teeth, or his life, Pine thought. He still carried his dagger in his coat pocket, but Dick Turpin's supposed confederate had only ever used the blade to help cut up pieces of tough meat on his plate.

Turpin could have looked and walked the other way. He could have argued that the dissembling rogue deserved his fate. But the highwayman was never keen on seeing a poor man being robbed. Turpin wasn't as sober as a judge (as judges were seldom sober) but he still had his wits about him. Enough to play a convincing drunk himself.

"George, is that you? It's Cormac. Come inside and have another drink," Turpin announced, slurring his words. His eyes were half-closed as he meandered towards the end of the alley, nearly stumbling over a crate as he did so. It was quite a performance. He only hoped rather than expected that his presence alone would scare the robbers away.

"Piss-off!" Butler stated unceremoniously, spittle freckling the air.

"Pardon?" Turpin replied, feigning difficulty in understanding the stranger, as he continued to advance towards the three men.

"I said…"

Before Butler could repeat himself, Turpin buried his boot in the man's groin. He doubled over in agony, his expression resembling someone about to retch. Tom Martin did not have the time to gather his thoughts and come to the aid of his friend. Turpin moved forward, whipping his elbow around to connect with his opponent's jaw. The highwayman proceeded to grab Martin's head and smash it against the wall, several times, before the brute collapsed to the piss-soaked ground. Turpin turned his attention to Butler once again, before the big man could rouse himself. Turpin picked up the nearest wooden box and smashed it over the bare-knuckle fighter's head, rending him unconscious. The attack was as sudden as it was ferocious. Turpin hoped that his clothes hadn't been stained with any blood, fearing a certain look or audible silence from his wife if she discovered any incriminating evidence.

Pine's mouth was agape, revealing a set of teeth as crooked as his nose. He placed his hand against the wall to steady himself. He wondered if he somehow knew the man who had saved him. Pine was unused to experiencing acts of courage or kindness. As much as he was keen to thank the good Samaritan, Pine was also eager to leave the scene, lest his adversaries come to again.

"Thank you. Here, I must give you something for your trouble. As you may have heard inside, this is very valuable," Pine said breathlessly, as he retrieved the dagger from his coat pocket. "It belonged to Dick Turpin. He's a friend."

Before the highwayman could refuse the gift, he found himself with it in his hands.

"I need to go, but you must first let me know your name," Pine asked, his voice still tremulous. Anxious or excited.

Turpin paused, wryly smiling to himself once more. On the cusp of laughing.

"You wouldn't believe me if I told you."

Turpin's Tax

"Being a good person doesn't pay," Samuel Tyler lamented, holding his head in his hands, drowning in regret. So much regret that the tavern owner had scarce time to feel embittered. The landlord of *The Silver Buckle* in Colchester had recently opened up his accounts to the new, local tax official. one Tobias Glutt.

Glutt had ordered him to pay a bill that would likely put him out of business. The official had leapt on any mistake and discrepancy, quicker than a politician would jump on an actress. Tyler had pleaded for the bureaucratic to be lenient - and discuss a way of paying the sum over an extended period of time - but Glutt would not be "corrupted". The martinet would do his duty.

"I do not make the rules, I only enforce them. Everyone needs to pay their fair share. The state's munificence must come at a price. Taxes are the lifeblood of government and the economy, keeping the body politic alive," the former university student, whose father had been a petty official in Westminster, had somewhat self-righteously argued.

Dick Turpin, under the guise of John Palmer (an honest landlord and the proprietor of a butcher's shop), listened to his friend and expressed sympathy for the predicament he was in, as they sat in *The Silver Buckle*. Turpin was tempted to offer to lend his fellow tavern owner the money to pay the punitive tax bill, but it would still be difficult for Tyler to dig himself out of the hole that Glutt had put him in. It was as deep as a grave.

The highwayman enjoyed coming to the establishment. Tyler was honest enough not to water the beer down, the food was good fare, the porter went down well and the serving girls were pleasing on the eye. As he looked around this afternoon, however, Turpin noticed that fewer candles and lamps were lit, less wood stoked the fire, the portions of food were slightly smaller and fewer serving girls were tending to customers. Tyler complained that he could no longer pay suppliers on time, where before he had prided himself on doing so. His credit and good name would soon no longer be what they were. Despair hung heavy on him, like a moth-eaten winter coat.

Over the past few months Turpin had visited *The Silver Buckle* more often. He met with Nicholas Pott at the drinking hole, the son of a housebreaker Turpin had worked with several years ago. Pott was entering the family business and the veteran criminal was taking the fresh-faced rogue under his wing and proffering some advice: "Make sure you plan ahead... Empty houses are low hanging fruit... Look after the tools of your trade and they will look after you. Make sure you trust any partner as you would your father or brother... Hopefully you will not make the mistakes I did, although you will still make some of your own," Turpin remarked, as he inwardly cringed and felt a shudder of guilt, recalling the grim events at Earlsbury Farm when he was a member of the Gregory Gang. The robbery had not been his finest hour.

Nathaniel Gill, Turpin's stout partner in crime, felt compelled to order more food and drink to support the landlord, after hearing his litany of woes - albeit Gill owned the appetite of a horse and would have devoured plenty of plates and jugs regardless.

Turpin listened intently to Tyler's difficulties. Thankfully, he experienced few money troubles. Not only was his wife, Elizabeth, a wonder in the kitchen - she knew how to cook the accounts for his businesses too. Tyler had been too honest. Honesty doesn't pay. Crime paid - which was another reason why Turpin could afford his lifestyle. The highwayman kept a room in London. He dressed and ate well. His wife never went without (not that Elizabeth wanted much). Nor did any mistress that the outlaw courted in the capital.

Turpin listened even more intently, however, when Tyler spoke about how, in a cruel act of irony, Glutt would be frequenting the tavern the day after tomorrow. The tax official would be accompanying half a dozen soldiers as they took the monthly tax revenues in a carriage to London. The highwayman's ears pricked up, like a dog whose master had just said "dinner time", when the landlord unwittingly disclosed valuable information about the potential score. The two highwaymen shared a covert but revealing glance - as both leaned in closer across the table, with Turpin even moving his measure of porter out of the way to do so.

"Glutt will be stopping off here at midday, along with the soldiers, before travelling on to Whitechapel. The peacock has asked me to put on a special lunch for him. And the parasite has even asked for a discount. They are all meeting here - the soldiers, coachmen and Glutt - to discuss their route. Apparently, there are three ways to get to Whitechapel - and they will settle on which one to take by drawing lots beforehand... Thank you John, for lending me your ear. I reckon I should leave you now gentlemen, before my bad luck rubs off on you," Samuel Tyler remarked, his voice as low as his spirits, before retreating into the kitchen.

"Well, what do you think?" Nathaniel Gill asked, licking his lips at the prospect of something other than food.

"I think it's time we gave ourselves a tax rebate," Turpin replied.

"Another porter?" a voice chimed in, as Polly Granger approached. Eyes bright and hips swaying. Polly had a broad smile and broader chest. Turpin had first encountered the serving girl around a year ago. He always tipped her well, after having tupped her one drunken evening.

"It would be rude not to," John Palmer replied, flashing a nigh on conspiratorial grin.

"She still seems fond of you," Gill stated, raising a suggestive eyebrow.

"I'll always have a tip for her, so to speak," Turpin responded, but he seemed pre-occupied. The highwayman was thinking. Planning.

"We could score so much coin that I might even be able to take Sally shopping in Piccadilly again. But we should not bite off more than we can chew. How are we going to deal with the soldiers?"

Turpin knitted his brow in concern. He had known other highwaymen to take on coaches guarded by a compliment of soldiers, but few lived to tell the tale. Soldiers were not afeared about shooting first and asking questions later. Some would be keen to shoot Dick Turpin too, to make a name for themselves. The odds of just two highwaymen subduing so many soldiers were close to impossible.

"I'm hoping that they won't have the stomach to travel to London by the time I'm finished with them."

The two men discussed the prospective score some more and then finished their drinks. The outlaws had homes and wives to get back to.

"Sally will have cooked for me," Gill said, beer dribbling down his chin as he rushed to leave after discovering how late it was.

"Will you be able to fit anymore in, after what you've just eaten?"

"I'll have to, otherwise my life won't be worth living. The things we do for love, eh?" the burly rogue remarked, affectionately patting his paunch.

24

Turpin was dressed in a brown, fitted woollen coat with russet breeches and smart, black riding boots. John Palmer appeared every inch a middling-class figure, as opposed to a working-class highwayman. As a stable hand passed him the reins of his mount, who seemed visibly pleased to see her master, a passing alderman commented:

"That's a fine horse you have there, a veritable Black Bess."

At the sound of her name the mare's ears twitched. Turpin smiled, both in receipt of the compliment and in wry humour.

***

Turpin spent the following day making certain arrangements. Although he was familiar with the county and the roads from Colchester to Whitechapel, he still obtained maps of the area to get a lay of the land. He visited Oliver Mortimer, an apothecary, who was not averse to concocting vials of toxins as well as medicine. Although the highwayman hoped not to use it, he also visited a local blacksmith to put a fresh edge on his sword. Towards the end of the day, he visited Colchester and *The Silver Buckle* once more, taking Polly Granger aside to have a quiet word with her, involving "a bit of business." He was fortunate enough to bump into Nicholas Pott too. Throughout the day, when conversing with various tradesmen, John Palmer asked about the new tax official in the county. It seemed that Tobias Glutt was making a name for himself - for all the wrong reasons.

"He's a zealot, a Grand Inquisitor, with his religion being the state," Oliver Mortimer explained. "The parasite is taking pleasure out of squeezing decent, hardworking people like a garotte. He recently closed down Molly and Henry's haberdashery. I also heard that he arranged for the government to seize the stock and premises of a dress shop in Harlow. A school, just outside of Colchester, may have to close soon too, as Glutt is applying the letter of the law and pursuing the establishment for unpaid taxes from five years ago. It's in desperate need now of funding and new pupils… It wouldn't surprise me if he is skimming or accepting bribes. Have you seen his house, or one might deem it a small estate? He's probably more corrupt than Walpole - and less pompous with it… I understand that he's fond of making speeches, preaching to those he's simultaneously condemning. Some men can rob you with a pistol in their hand, but some can do it with a pen."

To a staccato chorus of coughing, cursing and laughter in the background, Turpin tucked into some mutton chops and read a newspaper which another patron had kindly left on the table in the tavern. He hoped that there might be a piece by the journalist Samuel Johnson, who Turpin had the good fortune to have encountered more than once in the capital. The Scotsman had a pithy turn of phrase and was always worth reading. The highwayman recalled a few lines in the last couple of pieces he had read by Johnson:

"I never desire to converse with a man who has written more than he has read… Power is not sufficient evidence of truth… To be happy at home is the ultimate result of all ambition… What I gained by being in France was learning to be better satisfied with my own country."

Turpin didn't quite know whether to be amused or angered by some of the articles he read. Members of Parliament had voted to give themselves an increase in the payments they received for their selfless service to the country. They had also increased a subsidy to the East India Company, which Turpin was initially appalled by until he remembered that he had purchased shares in the venerable institution. Lord Devlin had awarded a lucrative government contract to a dockyard which was part-owned by his cousin. Another peer of the realm, Lord Lewin, had been caught having an affair with a leading Drury Lane actress. He explained that he was just trying to reach out and touch the thespian community, as they had touched him previously. Turpin read a theatre review, to find that a critic was enamoured with a new star. *"She shines like a diamond - brighter than the costume jewellery which adorned her... Miss Greene was unable to wholly conceal her West Country drawl, but thankfully she did not hide her comic timing under a bushel."* He was also somewhat amused to read how there had been a robbery by the infamous highwayman Dick Turpin just outside of Durham, which was news to the outlaw as he had never visited the area in his life. But journalists rarely let the truth get in the way of a good story.

"One cannot help but think, when one reads the newspaper, that the country is going to the dogs. We are certainly all barking, are we not?"

Roderick Stewart was a lawyer, from Islington, travelling on business to Colchester. He wore thick-lensed spectacles and a black outfit which would have befitted an undertaker. Pinched features. Chinless. Teeth as yellow as a Chinaman. Reedy, whining voice, as if his throat had been flattened by a mangle.

Turpin glanced up.

Having attracted the attention of his audience the lawyer, who liked the sound of his own voice as much as any politician, continued:

"Albion is in decline. Europe is a beacon of culture and civilisation, while our light diminishes. I sometimes think that our lower classes are little better than savages. One doesn't even need a newspaper to know that crime is on the rise. Gisly murders happen every day, to the point where they no longer shock. There seems to be more highwaymen lining our roads than hedgerows."

Commentators had been arguing how England was in decline for as long as there had been an England, Turpin mused. Most people who judged that England was an unhappy place were usually unhappy themselves, mired in envy and resentment.

"Our newspapers may build some of these wretches up to be the Robin Hoods of our day, but they are just common criminals. *Common* being the operative word," Stewart added, without waiting for a reply from the figure on the next table. "The rabble seem to love these outlaws. God help us if the bien pensant, or peasant, is ever given the vote in this country. We would go to rack and ruin even quicker, I warrant. God help us even more if the franchise is extended to women. I shudder to think," the lawyer posited, shuddering.

"I'm not so sure. Perhaps the fairer sex would help provide us with a fairer society, if they were enfranchised. But it might prove difficult to decide on a day to ballot them, when the majority of women are not feeling overly sentimental - or indeed hysterical," Turpin drily remarked, barely suppressing a smile.

"I am not sure how seriously I should take your humour, sir."

"That's fine. I cannot altogether tell when I am being serious or not either. I tend to leave politics alone. If only it would repay the same favour."

***

Turpin remarked to his wife, Elizabeth, the following morning that he may be home late that evening. He explained how he was due to meet with a farmer near Colchester, about supplying lamb for the butcher's shop. Elizabeth that knew her husband was lying (and not just because she had caught a glimpse of his pistol, cloak and mask in his black bag). And Turpin knew that she knew he was dissembling. But husband and wife were content to lie to themselves and believe that all was well. More remained unsaid than said. But perhaps that was the definition of a marriage.

The two highwaymen met at the turnpike and rode towards Colchester. Gill was carrying his own bag too, filled with a change of clothes and brace of pistols. They arrived at *The Silver Buckle* before midday and sat on the neighbouring table which Polly Granger had set aside for Glutt and his party. They ordered small beer and sipped their drinks, for once. The highwaymen needed to keep a clear head.

Tobias Glutt came through the door of the tavern around an hour after Turpin and Gill. The tax official was accompanied by four soldiers, and one coachman. The remaining soldiers and coachman kept watch on the coach and its valuable cargo outside. The soldiers, replete with carbines and swords, were tanned and flint-eyed. Other patrons in the tavern eyed them with wariness - and the soldiers watched them with suspicion in return. Turpin covertly took in the civil servant. He was plump, squat. His shirt buttons seemed fit for bursting beneath an expensive coat. The collar was open, allowing his toad-like throat to fit into the garment. Lank strands of black hair peeped out from beneath a powdered wig. Glutt carried an ornate, gold pocket watch. The prized possession not only kept good time, but it projected a certain status, the official judged. Black, furtive eyes betrayed the bile and resentment in his soul. Glutt had attended university, but he had finished bottom of his year. A worm slowly gnawed on his heart, as he considered himself a failure, believing that he a failure in the eyes of his peers and father. Most of his contemporaries at university had inherited capital or land. But Glutt had to toil for a living. It was unfair. But one day soon he would earn the rank and wage that was due to him. He would be promoted to the exchequer's offices in London, become eligible for an enviable pension and have staff working under him. He could afford to marry a woman of suitable quality and standing. He would also earn the respect of his father.

Turpin had arranged to be on the next table from Glutt to be in earshot of the official and soldiers. Yet such was Glutt's voluble tone that he could have heard most of what he said from across the street. He believed that he was somehow holding court, that his audience considered him important. The soldiers, who were just keen to wolf down their food and get on with their job, displayed a distinct lack of interest in what the self-regarding official was pontificating on, however.

"I am all too aware of how people say things behind my back and curse my name. There are folk who will attest to tax being a four-letter word. But they just need to be educated. Edified no less. Governments spend money wisely on the populace's behalf."

Turpin thought how he would much prefer to spend his money on his own behalf.

"People should be duly grateful for our government and its civil servants. Instead of hiding away when I come to call, I should be welcomed with open arms. Our government protects and provides. But such benevolence needs to be funded. Taxpayers need to realise that, rather than any of these wretched highwaymen, it is good servants of the state, like myself, who help to take from the rich to then re-distribute to the poor. Believe it or not but we can tax our way to prosperity. People just need to be more enlightened and have faith in the exchequer," Glutt proclaimed, before turning to hear a coughing sound emanate from the next table as one of the patrons seemed to be choking on his beer.

After discussing the route they would take to London a couple of the soldiers went from clasping their tankards to clutching their stomachs. Their tanned complexions turned ashen, albeit they were also green behind the gills. They looked like they were going to be sick - just before they dashed outside and were sick. Vomit splattered upon flagstones. They would also soon be able to shit through the eye of a needle. The stolid soldiers were barely able to stand or walk. Turpin almost winced in sympathy, observing the debilitated men. Thankfully another soldier in their party had recently popped into the tavern from waiting with the carriage outside. He too would soon be afflicted. The coachman had drunk from the same jug of ale as his companions. The poor soul was unable to reach the outhouse in time - and soiled his breeches. He shuffled back in, the soul of shame. The smell was as unwelcome as a tax increase. Glutt was alarmed and appalled. Patrons looked on, amused and repulsed by the pandemonium. Some peered at the table, trying to work out what the soldiers might have ordered - so they could avoid making the same mistake. Most customers had understandably lost their appetite, though.

Glutt asked the sergeant leading the soldiers if he should still proceed with the task of travelling to Whitechapel.

"Yes, you should continue. I won't be able to accompany you. My arse and innards feel like shit. Or are filled with shit," the soldier remarked, doubled over in discomfort. He was not alone in being incapacitated. Another soldier was tempted to complain to the landlord about the food or drink, but he didn't have the guts for it.

Glutt remarked that he understood the soldier's decision - and felt justified in his decision to drink wine instead of ale. The official promised himself that he would talk to the relevant authority about docking the pay of any soldier who did not fulfil their duty.

As Turpin and Gill took their leave to retrieve their horses, they were pleased to see that the herd would be thinned some more - as another soldier confessed that he was too ill to continue. As he sat over the toilet bucket, drenched in sweat, he asked for God to have mercy on his soul, or stomach. It was unlikely that God was watching over such an unseemly scene, however.

The money that Turpin had spent to purchase the toxin from Mortimer - and have Polly Granger serve it to the soldiers - had yielded a return. With only one soldier - and one coachman - to deal with, the impossible would now be probable, the highwayman surmised.

"You were right, Dick," Gill remarked as they left the tavern, grinning. "They don't have the stomach for the journey."

***

There was still work to be done. "There many a slip between a cup and a lip," Nathaniel Gill would sometimes say, or slur, after spilling his drink when drunk.

The highwaymen had changed, donning their masks and dark clothes. They sat on their large mounts. Ears flicked and tails swished from a congregation of insects passing by.

"You don't think that they've changed their route or given up on the trip, do you?" Gill asked his friend, impatient to start and finish the job.

"No," Turpin replied, with more confidence than he felt.

The two men were positioned at the heart of a stretch of woodland. A canopy of trees hung over the narrow road. Petals of dull light marked the damp, leaf-strewn track.

"It's always nice to be able to steal from a thief. That bastard has robbed more people than we have."

It was time for Turpin's ear to flick as he heard the distant sound of a carriage travelling along the rutted road.

Black Bess turned to her owner and nodded her large head, as if to convey that she was ready too. The outlaws concealed themselves behind the treeline. Darkness was ever the highwaymen's friend.

Just a young, solitary soldier accompanied the coach, which carried but one coachman and the tax official. Their pace was a fast trot or slow canter. The highwaymen let them pass but then soon gave chase by breaking into a full-bloodied gallop.

Gill closed in on the soldier riding behind the carriage. He wanted to get close to his target, to make sure his shot winged rather than killed the man. A flash of light could be seen within a cough of smoke, just before the ball grazed the soldier's right shoulder. The infantryman had no time to retrieve his rifle, as the brawny highwayman rode up to him and dragged the soldier from his mount. He fell to the ground, wounded and winded.

"Don't worry, keep your head down and your mouth shut - and this will all soon be over," Gill would soon be saying to his victim, whilst tying up his hands and feet. "Make sure you tell the newspapers that I was more handsome than Turpin – and a better shot," the masked outlaw added, with a playful wind.

As Gill's shot rang out, Turpin didn't flinch as he sped past the soldier and approached the carriage.

The perspiring coachman reached for the blunderbuss next to him, but as he turned to do so he observed two pistols being levelled at him.

"I'd prefer it if you could live to tell the tale of when Dick Turpin held you up," the highwayman amiably remarked, with the hint of a warning – speaking loudly enough to be heard behind his mask.

It was all seemingly over before it began, like a short story.

The coach slowed to a halt. Gill commenced to restrain the defeated, palled coachman as Turpin opened the door to the carriage.

"This is a government carriage," Glutt remarked, somewhat shrilly, as he stared down the barrel of the outlaw's pistol. The civil servant hoped that just by mentioning the word "government" the highwayman would be filled with either respect or dread. But, with his wig comically askew, it was the tax official who looked like he might soil his breeches, being poisoned by fear.

"I know, that's why I'm robbing it. I'm here to relieve you of your tax burden," Turpin cooly replied. His mask was pulled up high, his tricorn hat pulled down low. The usually eagle-eyed Glutt had no idea that the man climbing into the carriage to grab the strongbox was the same person who had been sitting on the adjacent table at the tavern. Thankfully, agents of the exchequer do not know or see everything.

***

John Palmer became a silent, unobtrusive partner in *The Silver Buckle*. Samuel Tyler was close to tears after hearing Palmer's offer and generous terms. He felt like his soul had been saved, rather than just his business.

"I'm not sure how I can thank you," the landlord declared.

"A measure of your porter will suffice, and you must allow my wife to go through your accounts before you submit your next tax return."

Samuel Tyler was not the only person in Colchester and its environs who started to believe in miracles that week. An anonymous donation was made to a school, which meant it could afford to keep its doors open. A haberdashery in Harlow took on a new partner, in the shape of one Nathaniel Gill, and announced in its window that it would soon re-open.

"It's time we gave something back, Nat," Turpin had argued. "It's in giving that we receive, as Francis of Assisi once said. Don't worry, there will still be plenty left over for us to enjoy ourselves. I'm still more of a sinner than a saint."

Gill agreed to his friend's proposal, but he duly thought to himself how being a good person didn't pay.

As for Tobias Glutt, he may altogether have started to believe in miracles, but he may also have been tempted to think about the concept of divine retribution. He returned home with a heavy heart after the robbery. It was with a heavier heart, however, that Glutt discovered he had been burgled. Most of his valuables had been purloined or destroyed. Nicholas Pott had been thorough, having been tipped off by his fellow thief that the owner of the property would be absent for most of the day. Pott cut Turpin in on the score and asked him to fence certain choice items of loot through Joseph Colman. As well as certain choice trinkets, Pott passed on a ledger he had found in a strongbox, concealed in the tax official's bedchamber. The ledger contained a record of the sums the administrator had skimmed (or the bribes he had taken) over the previous two years. Even more than Turpin and the reports of his misdemeanours in the newspapers, the tax official's crimes were in black and white.

Glutt's hand and heart trembled, after reading the note which was posted through his door a day after the robbery. The anonymous sender instructed the corrupt tax official that he was in possession of his damning ledger - and that Glutt should resign from his post. Otherwise the ledger would find its way onto the desk of his superiors in Westminster. His superiors were already somewhat peeved, as the tax revenues he was due to deliver had been earmarked to pay for a wage increase for their department. He slumped into his chair in his ransacked parlour. The walls, now devoid of paintings, felt like they were closing in. His hair would soon turn greyer than his powdered wig. He would rather resign than face eternal shame - and a prison sentence. He wondered how he might earn a living, let alone earn the respect of his father. Glutt held his head in his hands, not unlike how Samuel Tyler had done earlier in the week. It had been a taxing day or two.

Turpin's Mount

It was as pleasant a day as one could have hoped for in Essex, during September. Rich autumnal russets and browns adorned the landscape, along with ripe, soft greens and lustrous yellows - beneath a sky as blue as a robin's egg. The trees had yet to shed their leaves, the hedgerows were still teeming with life. A lone ploughman and shire horse could be seen toiling in a distant field - turning the earth. Even soil becomes exhausted and needs a rest and some care. The air was even free from the sickly-sweet aroma of manure which often perfumed such scenes.

Dick Turpin sat upon Black Bess, ambling along a track which looked down on the contoured, colourful valley. He was travelling home, in no particular hurry, from having lunch with his partner in crime, Nathaniel Gill. They had arranged a celebratory meal, after having a good month. Ill-gotten gains were still gains. Their bellies were now as full as their purses. Turpin's belt bit into his hips. The highwaymen had shared a large meat pie at *The Cock and Bull*. They had initially cut the feast in half but, as was their custom, Gill ended up consuming two thirds of the dish. Turpin had eaten a few oysters to start with, washed down with a measure of porter. Everything tasted better with porter, he believed.

"Food, glorious food," Gill pronounced, or almost sung, as he finally finished his meal. Satiated. Triumphant, at having bested the mound on his plate.

As was his habit, when he was alone with his horse, Turpin spoke to the creature. Aside from perhaps Gill and his wife, the highwayman spent more time with the mare than anyone else. He could have employed someone to do so, but Turpin still groomed and tended to his steed. Lest he arouse suspicion by calling Bess by her name too often, he had devised a series of whistles and trained her to respond accordingly, as in when to approach or stop. Turpin loved the loyal horse dearly - and not just because she had delivered him from capture on more than one occasion. It was difficult to remember a time when he had been without her.

"We're in a good place right now, Bess - and I am not just speaking about Essex. Elizabeth seems content too. Happy wife, happy life. I do not miss having a mistress - and I certainly do not miss the expense. It's exhausting, pretending to be fond of someone when you're not. It's equally exhausting pretending to be enamoured with someone who isn't fond of you. If ever some thoroughbred comes up and smells your arse - and whinnies exuberantly - know that he's only after one thing. Even when he's had his oats, he'll still want more. He may joke that there are no flies on you, or that one should never look a gift horse in the mouth - but trust him about as far as you can pick him up and throw him. Believe none of them. They are arrant knaves, all. Aye, you should trust him about as much as any journalist. The newspapers have been talking about me, or indeed us, again. I suppose it could be worse, they could not be talking about me," Turpin remarked, before waving his hand in front of his face, in an attempt to shoo some flying insects away - as he recalled some of the pieces that he had read in the past week. Wryly smiling. Amused (for the most part).

"The charming highwayman continues to live a charmed life. He remains one step ahead of the authorities, cocking a snook at them beneath his tricorn hat... And the people increasingly cheer him on and champion the elusive outlaw. As Robin Hood could disappear into the greenwood, Turpin has hideouts and confederates in every town and village

between Norfolk and London... One of his latest victims, the wife of a shipping merchant, described the highwayman as being "Tall, dark and handsome. He spoke French and quoted poetry to me, though it was difficult to know what he said and how he looked behind his black mask". It is unsurprising that other footpads and highwaymen are claiming to be Turpin when they commit their robberies, as they look to inspire fear or admiration. As many Dick Turpin's as there seems to be, popping up from Durham to Dungeness, there is only one Black Bess - although it is difficult to encounter any black horse now in Essex and beyond who isn't named Bess in honour of the outlaw's mount... There are some who believe that Dick Turpin died some time ago, and his name and persona were taken up by a gentleman who is living and loving a life of crime. Evidence suggests that he may be educated and genteel, a dandy - rather than lowborn. More virtuous than violent. More famous than infamous. "God bless Robin Hood," folk used to exclaim. Such is the appetite for stories about the highwayman, and his ability to help sell periodicals, that newspaper editors are doubtless saying "God bless Dick Turpin and Black Bess" every week."

Turpin was suddenly distracted from his half-idle, half-amused thoughts due to a figure walking towards him, along the narrow lane. Tall. Mid-twenties. Greasy hair. Greasier skin. The beginnings of a beard covered a narrow jaw and weak chin, which he often scratched as if afflicted with lice. The stranger was chewing on an unlit clay pipe and carrying a walking stick cut from a hawthorn tree. He was wearing a long, heavy coat which caused him to sweat - but he wouldn't be the first Englishman to misjudge the weather and wear the wrong clothing, Turpin judged.

"Good day to you," the young man amiably remarked, taking the pipe out of his mouth and placing it in his pocket.

"We are having some unseasonably warm weather. are we not? The sun can beat doubly down on one who is walking, compared to one who is riding. You have a fine mount there. She is a veritable Black Bess."

"Thank you," the highwayman replied, narrowing his gaze in scrutiny or suspicion.

"I am going to make you a trade, friend. You are going to give me your horse and in return I am going to give you a story you can tell down the tavern, about how you were robbed by Edmund Baldwin," the outlaw asserted, as he retrieved a pistol from his coat and cocked the loaded weapon.

Turpin sighed and rolled his eyes, appearing bored rather than frightened. He had heard the name before. Joseph Colman, the well-connected fence who Turpin dealt with in London, had mentioned the footpad in passing. Baldwin had come from the South-coast and had worked a variety of jobs - farmhand, docker, builder - before falling in with the wrong, or right crowd, in Portsmouth. Crime paid better than honest labouring - and Baldwin decided to make his way to the holy of holies. London was the Jerusalem of crime, although he joined the "Willis Gang" who worked throughout the county of Kent. The gang soon parted ways with their newest member, however. Rumour had it that they were appalled when Baldwin shot a ten-year-old boy, during a house breaking in Tonbridge. The highwayman also heard that Baldwin left the gang because they did not meet his ambitions - and the young man demanded a greater share of any loot. "Apparently he wants to be the next Dick Turpin," Colman explained, with the hint of a smile. For the past few months Baldwin had committed a series of robberies in Essex, including the murder of an elderly coachman.

Turpin was without his sword and brace of pistols. He was only armed with his wits. But his features hardened, and he stared defiantly at the robber. Instead of looking like he was about to be shot, Turpin glared at Baldwin like he wanted to injure him.

"Slowly dismount. And place the purse I see hanging off your belt into that saddlebag."

Edmund Baldwin licked his dry lips. The pistol shook a little in his hand. Turpin knew that his assailant had killed before and would not hesitate in pulling the trigger if he suddenly advanced. He would comply, up to a point. For now.

"I'll unhappily grant you the contents of my purse, but I should warn you about trying to take my horse," Turpin remarked, his voice as hard as obsidian.

"I'm the one holding the pistol, friend. I should be the one warning you."

"I know. You would think that."

A flicker of doubt, or even fear, barged into Baldwin's expression. A gust of wind blew through the leaves of the nearby birch trees, as if sensing the tension in the air. Black Bess grew jittery too, as the stranger clasped her reins. Her hoof scraped the ground and her head bobbed up and down as she whinnied. Agitated. The horse was wise enough to know something was wrong. Baldwin ordered the beast to be still and even struck its neck with his stick. Turpin winced at the blow, as if feeling the smart himself. He now stared at the footpad like he wanted to kill - rather than just injure - him.

"Tell your bitch of a horse to calm itself, else I'll put a bullet in its head, after putting one in yours," Baldwin threatened, worried that the mount might rear up at any moment.

41

Turpin caught the mare's eye and raised his palm, signalling to Bess that all would be well. Whatever was wrong would be made right. The horse grew calmer, almost immediately, trusting her master.

Baldwin leered, widely, in his victim's direction as the tall, one might even say gangly, young outlaw mounted the large mare easily. The former farmhand was experienced with horses. He was confident of making the handsome steed his own (he may even impersonate Dick Turpin with her, he fancied) - or he would earn a tidy profit selling the beast.

Black Bess snorted, with something akin to derision, as Baldwin dug his heels in her flanks, and she set off at a canter along the track. Kicking up a mulch of mud.

One might have imagined that Turpin would have appeared utterly distraught at witnessing a fellow outlaw ride off with his prized horse, that his frown would have increased in direct correlation to Baldwin's leer, but the highwayman wore a triumphant smile on his face, as if the contest was already over.

Two short whistles sounded through the balmy air, hammering out like a judge's gavel striking the block. The horse's ears flicked to attention. The powerful creature halted, throwing its rider forward, before then rearing up and throwing the stranger off - like a gorilla throwing a monkey off its back. The would-be horse thief fell in one direction, his pistol in another.

Baldwin was winded, prostrate on the track. He may have briefly lost consciousness. He squinted as he opened his eyes and felt a bruising pain from the top of his arse to halfway up his spine. The outlaw heard the damned horse whinny, albeit it now sounded strangely like laughter. Footsteps, crunching upon the ground, grew louder as

Turpin approached, pausing only to pick up the loaded weapon.

The highwayman stood over the footpad, his expression harder - and blacker - than obsidian.

"Forgive me friend, it was just a game," Baldwin feebly remarked. Attempting a conciliatory smile.

"Aye, a game you've lost."

"You go on. It's fine. Just leave me here."

"I will," Turpin replied. His hand shook not as he levelled the pistol in front of his opponent's petrified face and pulled the trigger. A spark fleetingly filled the air, along with a puff of smoke. Life turned to death in the blink of eye, with little or no explanation. Baldwin's countenance became a mulch of blood and bone. The dandy highwayman appeared less gentlemanly and genteel than the readers of certain newspapers would have imagined.

Black Bess was little troubled by the sudden shot, as she waited patiently for her master. Content, glossy and groomed. Swishing her tail. It was still a fine, clement day in many ways. Turpin patted the part of the mare's neck which Baldwin had struck.

"I'm not sure I do, but you deserve all the headlines you receive, girl," Turpin said wistfully, hoping that his wife hadn't cooked him a large meat pie too.

End Note

Should this be your first encounter with Dick Turpin then I hope this short book has whetted your appetite to read the series of novels I wrote. Should you have already read the trilogy then I hope that *Turpin's Tales* has been a satisfying, fun bonus coda.

Much like Robin Hood, fact and fiction had already been woven together before I got to add a chapter into the legend of Dick Turpin. Should you be interested in reading more about the real history behind the highwayman then I can recommend *Dick Turpin: The Myth of the English Highwayman* by James Sharpe.

Should you have enjoyed the Dick Turpin books, or any other series I have written, then do please get in touch via richard@sharpebooks.com

Thank you.
Richard Foreman.